Next of Kin

Dan Wells

ISBN 978-0692246030

Cover design by Chersti Nieveen.
Interior design by Ben Crowder.

www.TheDanWells.com

Published by Fearful Symmetry, LLC.

Printed in the U. S. A.

This book is dedicated to Ben Olsen, who told me to just let the bomb explode. Not in this book, in a different one—it's not like I'm going to put a spoiler right here in the dedication. Come on.

Acknowledgements

This book exists because of the hard work and invaluable expertise of many people, foremost among them my assistant, Chersti Nieveen, who offered suggestions on the manuscript, designed the cover, and handled a thousand other business-related tasks so that I could have time to write. The editing and proofing were done by Angela Eschler and Heidi Brockbank, and the production was carried out in a ridiculous rush—yet with flawless precision—by Christopher Bigelow, Eugene Woodbury, and Ben Crowder. Other helpful advice was given by Steve Diamond, Maija-Liisa Phipps, and my lovely wife, Dawn Wells.

Chapter 1

I DIED AGAIN LAST NIGHT.

His name was Billy Chapman, found in a snowbank in the streetlight shadow of a parking garage, and when I drank his memories, his death became mine. I remembered stumbling out of the bar, into the biting cold through a thick haze of booze; I remembered slipping on the ice and the sudden, sharp pain. I remembered all thirty-five years of Billy's life: his job and his boss and his car that didn't work and his wife Rosie.

Oh, Rosie. He loved her more than anything in the world, and with his memories, now so did I. And neither of us would ever see her again.

The police said we died of exposure, and that's common enough these days. In a good cold winter like this, most of my memories come from drunks who never made it home, or homeless wanderers who never made it anywhere. In warmer weather I die in other ways, but year after year, my story is the same. I live from death to death, sometimes two weeks, sometimes three, holding on as long as I can while my brain slips away like sand in an hourglass, grain by grain, loose and crumbling, until I can barely remember my own name and I have to find another. I drink their minds like a trembling addict, desperate and ashamed.

In the old days, I used to kill them myself, topping off my memory whenever and however I pleased, but those days didn't last long. The others called me a fool for loving them, these tiny mortals with their tiny lives, but they never understood that I was one of them now. That my mind contained a hundred thousand human selves, and whatever fragment was me—my true self—was lost forever in that overwhelming crowd. I've lived as a banker in Nebraska, as a soldier in the Confederacy, as a Portuguese sailor in the Age of Exploration. I wove silk in the ancient dynasties; I fought and died on the banks of the Nile. The memories sink and surface like flotsam, more painful every time. How can I kill my own heart? How can I hurt them when their joys become my own? So I wait for them to die, and then I drink in peace.

And my mind is full of death.

Sometimes I die peacefully, drifting away as I sleep. These are the easiest deaths, especially if I know it's coming, and my family is gathered close, and we talk and we laugh and we think about old times, and then I close my eyes and smile and dream. These are the easiest, but they are far too rare to count on. Most of my deaths are full of pain and fear: five endless, desperate seconds in a rolling car, or five agonizing months in a chemo drip and a painkiller cloud. I've even been murdered, more times than I can ever remember. Every time, though, every single time, the death itself is never the worst part. Leaving is never as bad as the people you leave behind.

Oh, Rosie.

*　　　　*　　　　*

I don't have many friends, as you might suspect. The people I know—or the people I think I know—don't know me, and I've learned from painful experience that those artificial links are best left alone. As for the others like me, the Gifted who can do the things I do, I have no time for them. I am neither human nor Gifted, and even the ones who share my disdain for the others' bloodlust—the ones who call us Cursed or Withered or Lost—don't really have a place in my gap-riddled mind. I avoid them as I avoid everyone else.

There is only one connection I keep, a man named Merrill Evans, and after drinking Billy Chapman's memories, I visited Merrill the next day. I often visit him after a death. The old man understands me, whether he realizes it or not. Either way, I owe him, and it's the least I can do.

I parked my car in the little lot behind the Whiteflower Assisted Living Center and went inside. It smelled like hand sanitizer and canned oxygen, and the air crackled with that impossible combination of reverent silence and too-boisterous laughter from nervous children, talking to loved ones in an exaggerated pastiche of the same conversations they had twenty years before.

"How are you, Dad? It's me, Brian, your son. No, Gordon's not here, that's your brother. He died thirty years ago."

"Hi Mom. I said, 'HI MOM, HOW ARE YOU?' Say hi, Maddy, but say it loud so she can hear you. MOM, THIS IS MADISON. Say hi, honey."

"Do you remember our old house on third? The biggest house in the neighborhood, and my mother kept it so clean. Did you ever go to that house? Oh, it was wonderful, with a wrought-iron gate and the most beautiful roses in a bright white trellis on the wall. Do you remember when you pricked your finger there?"

I stood at the reception desk, and the nurse smiled. "Hello, Mr. Sexton. How are you today?"

"I'm fine, thanks. How's Merrill doing?"

"I'm sure he'll be great now that you're here." Her voice was chipper, but a hint of sourness crept into it as she talked. "I wish his family visited as often as you do. Do you know he has three grandchildren? And his family almost never visits at all? The cutest little grandchildren you've ever seen. They were in here over the summer."

"I'm sure they come in when they can," I said.

"They could come more than they do," she said, shaking her head and picking up the phone. I put out my hand to stop her.

"Don't bother calling—he's not good over the phone. I'll just show myself up."

"That's fine," she said. "You know the way." She smiled, and I smiled back, but I only got a step away before she called after me.

"Mr. Sexton? Remind me again how you know Mr. Evans?"

"I met him once," I said, "not long before the... Alzheimer's. He was a good man."

"I'm sure he was," she said. She'd only worked here a few years, so she didn't know either of us well.

I turned again, my gaze rolling across the foyer full of visitors and residents and catching on one in particular: a teenage boy, skinny in his baggy coat, with ragged black hair that seemed almost deliberately uncombed; his own private rebellion against his mother or grandmother or whoever made him come in here today. He wasn't talking to anybody, just sitting in the corner, waiting. Expressionless. I longed, sometimes, for that lack of feeling. It would make so many things so much simpler.

Whiteflower was one of the new-style Assisted Living Centers, more like a hotel than a hospital. Merrill Evans lived in room 312; a dark red vase sat on the shelf outside his door, a sort of mental hook to help the residents find their rooms when they couldn't remember the number. Merrill got the vase on a trip to San Francisco with his wife, and he remembers it sometimes. I knocked on his door and waited while he shuffled close enough to yell out.

"Who's there?"

"It's Elijah." Not my real name, but the one I've been using the last twenty years or so. The only one he'd know me by, if he knew me at all.

"Who?"

So he didn't know me today. "I'm your friend, Merrill. I've come to talk to you."

"All my friends died in Vietnam."

What little he remembered changed from day to day; today it looked like he remembered the war. "You fought in the Tet Offensive," I told him. "I fought there, too." It wasn't even a lie.

He grumbled and opened the door, but his wrinkled face scowled when he saw me. "Hell, you didn't fight in 'Nam. You weren't even born yet."

"I have a young face," I said, which wasn't technically a lie either. I'd looked about forty years old for centuries.

Merrill grumbled some more but opened the door. "Nothing else to do around this place," he said, and walked back to his recliner, slowly but steadily. His mind was gone, but his body was still strong; he was sixty-five years old, younger than most of the residents in the building, but early onset Alzheimer's was common enough, and he couldn't take care of himself, so here he was. Healthy as a horse, empty as a drum.

"Did you bring my lunch?" he asked.

"I'm afraid not," I said, closing the door behind me and picking up his phone. "Would you like me to order some?"

"If you don't have my lunch, then why are you here?"

And thus began the slow spiral of conversation. "I'm your friend. I came to talk to you."

"That's right," he said, waving curtly with his hand, as if wiping grime from some invisible window. "I remember, you just said that." His words held a mixture of embarrassment and anger, the latter caused by the former. He knew he couldn't remember anything, and he hated it; he was ashamed and embarrassed and angry at everything in the world—himself most of all, for who else could he blame? It was the most heartbreaking gesture in the world, the most painful tone of voice to ever hear, but it was one of the primary reasons I came here. Three weeks from now, as the sand in my mind leaked relentlessly away, I'd make that same gesture, say that same thing. *I remember.*

The biggest lie in the world.

I worked in the morgue, driving the hearse during the night shift, because it was the best way to stay in constant, non-suspicious access to the recently dead. It was steady work, and if it kept me out of contact with the rest of the world, no matter. So much the better, really. I closed my blinds and slept by day, and by night I worked in the garage, maintaining our three hearses, keeping them clean and ready. The man on the day shift was nice enough. His name was Jacob, and I talked to him sometimes as I arrived for work and he was leaving. Sometimes he got sick and asked me to cover his shift, but I always made other arrangements, even paying for a temp out of my own pocket. I knew too many of the dead, and I knew their families, and I couldn't bear to see them weeping over me when I was right there, alive and well, and why are you crying over me? Let's leave this place and never come back. My own wife and children and parents and friends, as real in my memories as they ever were in the memories of the dead. I'd never gone to my own funeral, but I knew the temptation to talk to loved ones would be strong, so I stayed away.

That's why it was such a shock, one week after Billy Chapman, when I saw Rosie at the grocery store.

My cart was full—cucumbers and olives and capers and feta, for I had brushed past a sheepskin coat in the aisle, and I remembered my days on Crete with such crystal, visceral clarity it brought me to tears, and I wanted a meal like we ate in the old days. I was walking to the checkout, wondering if it would taste right—if the American ingredients would hold the same flavor, or if my memory of some magical ur-salad would overpower any real salad I tried to recreate—when suddenly there she was, arriving at the line at the same time I did, as familiar by my side as she'd always been, and I said hello without even thinking about it. She nodded back, friendly but distant, with a sadness in her eyes that broke my heart. I opened my mouth to ask what was wrong before I remembered that her husband was dead, poor Billy in the ground not three days, and it wasn't me who remembered her but him, and she didn't know who I was. My hand was already reaching toward hers, and I pulled it back in terror.

Rosie, right here, real and physical and *right here*.

"Are you okay?" Her voice was lilting and sad and concerned—so like Rosie to feel concerned for others when she was already in so much pain herself. I'd heard that voice in lazy mornings, in joyful songs, in cries of passion, in heartsick wails that we could never have children. I loved that voice, but it wasn't for me, and I felt like a voyeur even thinking about it, yet I couldn't stop. I tried to speak but I couldn't say a word, and she asked me again, "Are you okay?" I knew I had to speak or she'd just keep talking. I wanted to let her, but I knew it was wrong.

"I'm sorry," I said, pulling my cart backward. "Please, you go first. I'll find another checkout."

"You're very kind," she said, and I tried to smile, but I had to turn away to hide the tears in my eyes.

My Rosie, who was never truly mine. I left the cart in the next aisle, and then I left the store, walking slowly so I wouldn't make a scene. Her car was there in the parking lot, the same color I'd seen a hundred times, the same bumper sticker I'd begged her not to get, the same box of tissues that had been in the rear window for years. I turned and walked the opposite direction, leaving my car, stumbling through the ice, part of me crying out to go back to her and the other part insisting that no, I could never see her again, she wasn't really my wife, there was nothing I could do. What could I possibly say? "Hi, you don't know me, but I've known you for ten years, and I was married to you for eight, and I'm your husband, I'm Billy, I'm so sorry I went away." She'd call the police. She'd mace me and run and scream that I was a maniac, that I was a stalker, that I was a psychopath. I loved her too much to do that.

I wandered the streets for two frozen hours, shivering in my coat, watching the streetlights through the snow. When I went back for my car, she was gone.

A week later I couldn't find my keys, and I knew it was starting. It's a simple enough thing, to lose your keys, but I recognized the signs, and I knew that the sand was slipping away from the hourglass. Short-term memories went first, but even the long-term memories would disappear if I waited too long. I felt like Merrill sometimes, now and then forgetting even who I was but remembering, out of nowhere, some ancient event or person I hadn't thought of in centuries. I had long ago forgotten my original self—anything I had left was cobbled together from the few memories that remained, an ever-shifting set of touchstones and anchor points that was all I had left of a real identity.

When I found the keys, I pulled my lanyard from the side-table drawer and clipped them to my belt. I made myself a lunch to take to work, sealing it carefully in a plastic container, and when I opened my bag to put it in, I saw another plastic container already sitting there, not thirty minutes old. I put a note on the second lunch, explaining its existence to my future self, and left for work. I said hello to Ted, and he told me his name was Jacob, that Ted had quit two years ago, and I apologized for the slip.

"Of course. I remember."

I'd chosen this city for its size: big enough to have a steady flow of the dead, but small enough that most of those bodies came from natural causes. I've died of heart disease more times than I can count. The death rate in our county is around 10,000 per year, which is just over 27 per day; about half of those are in the city itself, shared between two dozen morgues and mortuaries, which gives mine a new body every five or six days on average. We'd had one the day before, but I'd chosen to wait. I wasn't bad yet, and the woman had drowned, which is a death I try to avoid when I can. My memory always seemed to erode faster toward the end, though, and I would need to drink the very next mind that came through.

I ran through my maintenance checks on all three hearses, finding solace in the comfortable routine of reading lists and checking boxes. It was simple, the same routine every time. There was nothing to remember, so I had nothing to forget. When I finished, I sat in the office doing Sudoku, folding the little paper book in half and licking the tip of my pencil like an old man. Logic problems and strategy games are supposed to be good for memory retention, exercising your brain like a muscle, but I don't know if I've ever seen any benefit from it. I don't even know if the standard rules apply to my neurochemistry. I'd been doing Sudoku for so many years, I doubt it would exercise my brain at all anymore, regardless; it was an action as rote as the checklist on the hearses. When the phone rang I sighed in relief, took careful notes on where to pick up the new body, and left.

Another drunk, homeless this time. They found his body next to an overpass, fifty feet or so from the nest of blankets that was probably his home. It was several degrees below freezing, and his body bore no signs of attack, so they ruled it another accidental death by exposure.

His memory told another story.

His name was Frank McClellan, and he grew up in California; we walked on the beaches as a child, barefoot and tan, but we had never liked our father and the memories of our screaming arguments burned like coals inside my skull. We'd left home at sixteen, traveling here and there around the country, reconnecting with our sister for a few years in our twenties before drifting away again. Eventually we'd fallen into drugs and prostitution, though we'd always been proud that we'd stayed away from theft and robbery. I felt his pride, and his loneliness, and the bone-aching chill that seemed to haunt him even in the summer, and then last night I watched a man approach us—his face nearly buried in a thick, black scarf—and gesture to the shadows with a wad of dollar bills. We followed him, knowing exactly what was wanted in the wordless transaction, and there in the darkness he killed us.

The killer was one of the Gifted.

It was no surprise the police hadn't seen anything, for this Gifted had been careful to leave no trace. Frank hadn't recognized the dark, slick tendril reaching out from the folds of the man's scarf, but I did. It was like a twig of withered soul, black as the pit of Hell, and it reached through Frank's mouth and down his throat to pierce his heart. If someone got suspicious enough to do an autopsy—and somehow convinced the state that a nameless drifter was worth the money—they'd find his inner organs sliced or ground or pureed, maybe even missing completely. I knew the method as surely as I knew my own, the knowledge coming not from Frank's memory but from my own. There were too many holes in it to recall the details—too many thousands of lifetimes to ever have hope of keeping them sorted. I didn't know who this Gifted was, but I knew what he did, and I knew how. And I was deeply, unfathomably terrified.

I pondered on Frank's killer for the rest of the night and all the next day, too agitated to sleep. There weren't supposed to be any other Gifted in this area—I had chosen my home based on solitude as well as sustenance. The more I thought about it, the more I focused my newly heightened thoughts on the image of the killer, the more certain I became that Billy Chapman had seen the same man right before he died. He'd fallen on the ice, already unconscious by the time the monster took him, but he had seen him first, in the darkened streets and in the bar before that. This was not a pair of random deaths, and it was not an errant killer passing through. There was a monster stalking our shadows, gaining in power and boldness, and the deepest dungeons of my rat-gnawed mind cried out in horror at his coming.

I thought about going to the police, but what would that accomplish? I couldn't tell them what was happening without looking crazy, and I couldn't tell them how I knew about it without looking crazy *and* dangerous. I'd lose my job at the very least and face stiff fines and charges at the worst, possibly even ending up in jail. Either way, I'd lose access to the memories I needed to fuel my mind. In prison, I'd have to kill or lose my memory completely, a harrowing experience that could last decades and risk exposing my secrets to the world. If I lost my job, I'd have to leave town, and who knows how long it would be before I could find another ready source of memories.

Besides, I couldn't risk leaving, because that would mean leaving the killer alone with Rosie. I loved her more—

—Billy loved her more—

—I didn't know how to think. I hadn't seen the people I remembered, up close and in person, in years. In centuries, maybe. I had grown complacent, letting my careful measures grow lax; now I'd seen Rosie, and I couldn't leave her. I loved her as much as Billy ever had, for all his love was mine now, but now that I'd seen her, *I* loved her too, myself, whatever shreds of me remained inside the scattered library of my brain. Leaving her alone—with a killer on the loose—was unthinkable.

Protecting her, I knew, would be just as bad.

*　　　*　　　*

I don't know if I arranged my next meeting with Rosie or not. I didn't actively try to find her, but I didn't try to avoid her, either. I knew where she lived, and where she worked, and where she shopped; I knew all her friends and her relatives. These things and more were the cold remnants of a life that wasn't mine, but that didn't make them any less prominent in my memory. I could have gone to her gym, but I didn't; I could have followed her on her runs through the park, but I didn't. I'm not a stalker. But we shopped at the same grocery store, and I didn't change this habit, and sooner or later, perhaps inevitably, we met again.

She spoke to me this time, in the pallid light of the bright fluorescent bulbs. "Hi."

I looked up, not surprised or resigned or scared or sad but somehow all of them at once. I tried to hide it. "Hi."

"Are you all right?" she asked. She was always so concerned about people. "I saw you in here last month."

"I remember."

"You looked..." She paused. "I don't know, like maybe you needed help. Is there... anything wrong?"

Everything and nothing, I thought. I smiled, but only faintly, for I knew that everything I was doing was wrong. "That's very kind of you," I said. "I'm fine, though."

"Are you sure? I don't want to pry, and I know it's none of my business, but..." She hesitated. "Well, I just lost someone very dear to me, and when I saw your face, I thought... well, I guess I thought I recognized something."

I clenched my teeth, biting down on the joy that threatened to burst up through my chest—that she knew me, that she remembered me—but I knew that couldn't be true, and I waited for the next words that tumbled out in a helpless rush.

"I thought I recognized a little of myself," she said, "of my grief, I guess you could say, and I thought maybe here was somebody else going through the same kind of pain I was going through, and maybe he had someone to share it with and maybe he didn't, and I'm certainly not a poster child for quality grief management, but at least I have someone to talk to, I have my sisters and my parents and my in-laws, and maybe I'm completely off base with this and I'm seeing things that aren't there, and you're probably wondering who this psycho is that's trying to dump all this angst on you right here in the produce section, and I'm sorry to even bother you—"

"I lost someone too," I said softly. Not just Rosie, but a hundred thousand more. "I'm okay, though," I said. "I'm not... whatever."

"Are you sure?" asked Rosie. She could never stop herself from helping any sick neighbor or broken-winged bird that crossed our path, and I felt a sharp pang of guilt that I had somehow arranged this, that I had known her foibles and attracted her on purpose, even subconsciously.

I nodded. "I'm fine."

She looked at me a moment, and I wondered if I had made it through another encounter without ruining my greatest love's life, and if that meant she was going to leave me now, again, and I cursed myself for wondering which would be worse. Better to ruin my own life a thousand times than to hurt her any more than my death already had. But I didn't move, and I didn't speak, and then she did: "Who did you lose?"

"My wife."

"I'm so sorry." She put a hand on my arm, and I felt myself die all over again. I held myself still, as long as I could, but it was too much, and I pulled away. She looked at me with renewed pain in her eyes. "Do you have other family? Someone to talk to?"

"I get by," I told her, but it wasn't a real answer, and she knew it. She thought for a moment, pursing her lips in that way she does, so familiar I could wrap myself in the gesture like a warm, soft coat.

"I'm in a counseling group," she said. "Like a group therapy thing, but not as hippy-dippy as that probably sounds." She dug in her purse for a card while she spoke but found nothing and finally wrote the address on a scrap of an old receipt. "If you need to talk to someone, about anything, we'd love to have you. Everyone there is so nice, and I think it might—well, I know it's helped me. It's still helping me." She held out the paper. "Please come."

I had rules to follow. Traditions that had kept me safe, along with all the people I loved. *The lives you take are not yours to live. The people you miss aren't yours to miss. Don't talk to them, don't tell them the truth, don't tell them anything. Remember them because you have to, but no more. Don't follow them, don't hurt them, don't drag them into the hell of your own impossible life.* But there was a killer in town, now—a Gifted, a Cursed, a Withered. I wanted to protect the woman I remembered as my wife.

I had followed these rules for thousands of years, but I would break them all for Rosie.

I took the address. "Thanks. I might."

*　　　　*　　　　*

"Meshara."

I looked up from my puzzle book to see a man standing in the doorway to my small office in the morgue's garage and two more men behind him in the hall. The word they used was familiar and unfamiliar at the same time; one of the many things I'd learned and forgotten in my vast, patchwork life.

"I assume that's a name?" I asked.

"Typical," said the man, walking in and sitting down in the other chair. He was improbably handsome, but pulsing with feral power, like a hyena disguised as a god; the kind of killer that could easily bring down a healthy antelope but chose instead to tear the sick ones to pieces. He grinned, showing off his teeth as if to complete the metaphor in my head. "Understandable, though, isn't it? I think the phrase is: You've forgotten more than the rest of us have ever learned."

"All of us but Hulla," said one of the other men. He was taller and broader, with a web of scars across his face that sparked a distant, unformed memory. The third man was whip-thin and silent.

The Gifted had come for me.

"Hulla doesn't even go by that name anymore," said the first man, leaning back in his chair. "Calls herself 'Nobody.' Can you believe it?"

"*Called*," said the second man.

I sighed and closed my book. "Not all of us like those old names," I said. "Elijah's good enough for me."

"It shouldn't be."

"I can't even remember who I was back then," I said softly.

"I certainly can't remember my name."

"Meshara," he said again. "And I'm Gidri, and this is Ihsan and—"

"You know I really don't have any interest in your little . . . Gifted club, or whatever it is." I shrugged, not really sure what else to say. "I said as much to the last one, whatever his name was, when he came here a few years ago. Forman, I think? Nothing's changed since then. If anything, it's changed in the other direction, and I'm less likely to join you now than I was."

"Kanta," said Gidri, "or Forman, as you insist on calling him, is dead."

I straightened, feeling the import of his words like a blow to the head. "He is?" I looked at the tall man—Ihsan, Gidri had called him. "And you said . . . Hulla, as well?"

"And Mkhai," said Gidri. "And Jadi. And, as of last week, Agarin."

"Agarin was . . ." I tried to remember, struggling against the void in my mind. "She was a healer."

"In name only," said Gidri, "and not for centuries. Most recently she worked as a nurse, right here in your own city." He grinned again, flashing his yellow teeth. "If you've picked up any infant bodies from the hospital, you've seen her work."

I shook my head, sickened by the thought. "I had no idea."

"That's the whole point," said Gidri. "She was lying low, just like you are, just like all of us are, but that's not working anymore. They're fighting back now."

"Who is?"

"The humans." Gidri said the word with a wicked blend of disgust and excitement, the way one might refer to a dogfight. A creature worth nothing but scorn had surprised him with its competence, and he was practically giddy at the violent implications. He sat up straight in his chair, leaning forward with tightly coiled strength. "They've hated us as long as they've known about us, or at least as long as they haven't been worshipping us, but now they're fighting back— not just one, here and there like they used to, but organized.

A concerted effort of extermination."

"Kanta organized you first," I said. "He attracted too much attention."

"If it wasn't for Kanta, we wouldn't even have known they were hunting us," said Gidri. "How long have you been alone? How long since any of us had any goals at all beyond our basest instincts to hide and survive? For all we know they've killed dozens more—there are still so many Gifted we haven't even found yet."

"Well, you've found me, and I'm alive," I said firmly, reopening my Sudoku book. I glanced nervously at the third man, whose name I hadn't heard and who had thus far remained silent. He stared back, unmoving, and I looked at my book uncomfortably. "Go back and tell the others I'm fine, and while you're at it, tell them to leave me alone."

"You're one of us."

"In name only," I said, echoing their description of Agarin. "I've always been closer to the humans than to you, even since the beginning." I looked up. "You keep yourselves apart from them, but I can't. I know them too well—I've been them more than I've been myself." I shook my head firmly. "I wouldn't join Kanta, and I won't join you."

"They are hunting us," Gidri hissed. "Do you love them enough to lie down and let them kill you?"

"I..." I started and stopped, unsure what to say. "The more you kill, the more they'll see of us, and the more they see, the more they'll hate us. You're starting a war that can only end one way."

"With godhood!" he shouted, slamming his fist on the desk. He lowered his voice and hissed through clenched teeth. "They used to worship us, Meshara—they used to worship you. The god of wisdom, the god of beginnings, the god of dreams. They chanted your name in the darkness, dancing naked around the first fires of the ancient world, and now you're here, hiding and tired and worthless, as scared of living as you are of dying."

"Maybe it's time for us to die," I said, though my voice was weak. I didn't want to, but his description gave me pause. What was I really living for? After thousands of years and the reigns of kings and the rise and fall of civilizations—why was I still here, when I had no plans beyond the next dose of memory? If my only ambition was the absence of death, was that really a life?

I remembered the hopes and goals and dreams of a numberless host of humans. I remembered nothing of my own. I hadn't wanted anything for as long as I could remember . . . until Rosie.

"War is coming," said Gidri, "whether you want it or not, and with it comes death: yours, or theirs."

"You're talking about the end of the world," I said.

"Now you understand," said Gidri. "Either we die, or we reclaim our place as gods."

Ihsan's voice was deep and ominous. "Guess which one we're choosing."

The third man, sharp-faced and sinister, merely watched me from the corner.

*   *   *

"Who's there?" asked Merrill.

"It's me, Elijah. I'm your friend."

"I have friends?" He unlocked the door, and his face was etched with worry. "Come in here, where they can't hear you."

I stepped inside, wondering what new paranoia was worming its way through his brain.

He closed the door quietly, locking it behind him with fumbling fingers. "Do you know where my house is?"

I gestured around at his room. "This is your home, Merrill."

"This place?" He looked at me with wide eyes. "I don't live here. I live in a house! I need to get back there, or the neighbors'll start complaining."

"There's nothing for anyone to complain about."

"Have you seen the snow out there?" He shuffled to the window, pulling open a gap in the slats of the blinds. "I need to get home and shovel the walks, and these people won't let me."

"Your son is shoveling the walks," I assured him, though it wasn't true. His family had sold his old house to help pay for Merrill's care—augmented secretly by my own payments. It was the least I could do. But I'd learned over the years that any talk of selling his house worried him, even more than not knowing where his house was; there was a link somewhere, buried in his mind, that tied him to the *idea* of his home more strongly than to the home itself. It was the work, I think, not the bricks or the mortar, but the effort he'd put into maintaining them. As long as he thought someone was taking care of it, he'd eventually forget about the whole thing. Until another snowstorm brought the memory gasping to the surface.

I sat down, hoping the sight of me relaxing would help him to relax as well. "How have you been, Merrill?"

"They won't tell me anything in here, and they won't let me leave." He looked at me with a mix of suspicion and embarrassment. "Did you say you're my son?"

"I'm your friend, Merrill. My name's Elijah."

"Then who's my son?"

"Your son is named David."

"And he's taking care of my house?" He could get so fixated on things.

"Of course he is. Have a seat, Merrill. Tell me about your day."

He looked at the door and whispered loudly, "Do you think you could get me out of here?"

I sighed, but nodded. "Not out of the building, Merrill, you know that, but I can take you for a walk around the halls."

"I don't want to walk around the halls," he said bitterly. "I don't even know what this place is."

"You live here." I stood up. "Let's go for a walk."

"And good riddance." He started fumbling with his jacket—not a heavy coat, like he'd need outside; I didn't even think he had one. I took the light jacket from him and draped it over my arm.

"Let me hold that for you." I opened the door and closed it again behind him as he shuffled out into the hall.

"I hate this place," he said, brushing past the red vase on his hallway shelf. He looked at me with a sudden twinkle in his eye, as if the simple act of passing through the door had changed his mood. "Too many old people." He chuckled, and I laughed with him. We walked down the hall, slowly but smoothly, and waited at the elevator. "Where are we going again?"

"Just down to the lobby for a walk around the halls."

"You should have left your coat in my room," he said, pointing at his jacket on my arm.

"I don't mind carrying it."

The foyer was busy, at least for this place. A handful of families sat here and there on couches and chairs, chatting with their mothers and grandmothers, old men and women in wheelchairs and walkers, with oxygen tanks, plastic cannulas draped over ears and faces like translucent alien jewelry. Merrill's face brightened when he saw the foyer, and that recognition was as sad to me, in its way, as the confusion he'd had in his room—not because I didn't want him to be happy, but because of the speed with which he moved from one emotion to the other. He hated this place, and he wanted to get out, and after one door and one hall and one elevator, he'd forgotten it all. He was here in a place that he recognized, and it didn't matter that he hated it because that glimmer of recognition overshadowed every other emotion. Here was something he remembered, somewhere he'd been before, and just like that, he was happy. He smiled and waved to someone he'd probably never met, and I walked behind him with the jacket he'd forgotten.

"Does this place have a restroom?" he asked, and I pointed him toward a door in the wall. He shuffled in, and I sat down to wait. A young man was sitting on the couch across from me, someone I thought I recognized, but I couldn't be sure. Thin, maybe seventeen years old, with a ragged mop of dark black hair. He was alone, with a dead, emotionless expression, and I remembered Rosie's concern for others, the way she'd sought me out in the grocery store, and I leaned forward.

"Here for a grandparent?" I asked.

He looked at me, his face unreadable. "Kind of."

"Kind of a grandfather, or kind of a grandmother?"

"Friend of a friend."

I nodded. "I suppose you could say the same for me."

He said nothing and turned back to staring into space. I thought about Rosie again, and the way she'd talked to me, and the buried pain in this boy's face. I spoke again. "Are you okay?"

He looked at me with a new expression—not an emotion but a calculation, as if he were trying to figure out who this intrusive stranger was and why said stranger thought it was okay to ask such probing questions out of nowhere. It occurred to me how dangerous my question was, not physically but socially, for the most likely response was almost guaranteed to be an attack: he'd ask what my problem was, or tell me to stop bothering him, or simply get up and leave. I waited, trying to form some kind of defense or explanation, but he simply watched me, saying nothing. After a moment he glanced over my shoulder, nodding at the restroom.

"Who's your friend?"

"Just some guy," I said, surprised by the question. "I met him about twenty years ago, right before the Alzheimer's. It's not really Alzheimer's, actually, but it's close enough. He was a good man, and I liked him."

"And now you still visit him."

"It's the least I can do."

The young man's eyebrow went up, just slightly—the first hint of emotion he'd displayed. "I'm sure you could do a lot less if you put your mind to it."

It was a joke, of sorts, and I chuckled, but more at the joke's sudden appearance than at its meaning. It made me feel suddenly dark, like a chill wind had blown through the foyer. "You'd be surprised how little of my mind there is," I said, shaking my head. "Another few years and I'll end up like Merrill, more than likely, just a...hollow man. An organic machine, going through the motions."

"So is it worth it?"

For the second time in our short conversation, his question stopped me cold. I looked at the boy in surprise. "Is what worth it?"

"Coming here," he said. "Caring about a man who doesn't care about you—who couldn't care about you if he tried. Making connections with people who are only going to disappear."

I wondered what had happened to this boy to jade him so thoroughly, but then I shook my head. We were sitting in a rest home, surrounded by the last brittle gasps of a hundred dying lives. If he knew one of them, if he'd watched them fade from a vibrant human being to a distant, shuffling figure—if he'd listened as an old, familiar voice forgot his name—that was all the answer I needed. He was broken, because life had broken him. I recognized this boy, because I recognized that broken expression every time I looked in a mirror.

I looked down at my belt, at my keys clipped securely to my lanyard, and I saw myself in Merrill's room. In Merrill's life. Who would visit me when I finally lost it all? Who would help me pick up all the pieces of my shattered mind and console me when it snowed and I remembered some distant, unshoveled sidewalk? Who would knock on my door and call himself my friend?

Rosie had spoken to me in the grocery store. She saw me once, for half a second, and she remembered and she looked for me and she found me again, weeks later, and she offered to help.

The restroom opened, and Merrill came out, and I knew that I was already gone from his memory. I could walk out the door right in front of him and he wouldn't even know he'd been left. I looked at the boy, but he was already looking away, staring at the wall. I stood and turned toward Merrill.

"All set?"

"Well, look who's here," he said brightly, his standard phrase when he reacted to someone who obviously knew him, to hide the fact that he didn't know them back.

I held out his coat. "You still want to go for a walk?"

"I can't go for a walk. Have you seen the snow outside?"

"There's certainly a lot of it."

He stared out the front door, deeply concerned about something. "Who do you think shovels all that stuff?"

"They have a man they pay to do it," I said, taking him by the elbow. I have touched so few people in my life, almost none of them living. I pulled my hand away with a sudden rush of guilt.

"Do I live here?" he asked softly.

"You do. Would you like to go back to your room?"

"Do you know the way there?"

"I do." I gestured toward the elevator, and we started walking.

It was the least I could do.

*　　　　*　　　　*

Rosie's grief counseling meeting was held in a community center, in a suburb outside of the city. The room was used for all kinds of different activities, I guessed, looking at the posters and the bookshelves and the ill-cleaned tables from a pottery class. There were five people there, sitting on folding chairs in a loose circle in the center of the floor. They all looked up when I peeked in, and Rosie's eyes lit up when she saw me. My heart swelled in response, but I stayed quiet and moved slowly. I wasn't here to talk to her, but to stay nearby in case the Gifted came looking for trouble. Were they likely to? Not here, I knew, not this far from everything, but where else could

I protect her? It was the least I could do.

I thought about the boy from the rest home, and I knew I could do more. Was it worth it, making connections with people only to have them disappear? I had to make sure Rosie didn't disappear.

"Come in," said Rosie, beckoning with her hand, and I opened the door wider. She stood and pulled another chair into the circle, and I hesitated a moment longer in the doorway. It would be best if I left now and cut off all of my communication with Rosie. I could protect her just as well from the shadows, waiting outside and following her home, but then she took a step toward me, just a single step, and I couldn't help myself. I walked into the room. She gestured to the chair, and I sat in it gingerly, as if expecting at any moment for the room to erupt in chaos and terror and death.

All was still.

"Welcome to our group," she said, smiling softly. "My name is Rose. Would you like to introduce yourself?"

I almost said Billy—it was on the tip of my tongue—but I caught myself. I knew I should leave, but I took a slow breath. "Elijah," I said. "Elijah Sexton."

"Hello, Elijah," said Rosie. "Thank you for coming today. This is a very open group; most of what we do is just talk, and we've all gone through some of the same hard experiences, so you'll find us to be a pretty understanding audience. You told me before that you'd lost someone. Would you like to talk about it?"

I looked around at the others in the group: a middle-aged woman with a wide, grim face; a tall, skinny man behind a pair of thick black glasses; a pair of older people that looked like a couple. It struck me suddenly that I knew them all— that every one of the people in this grief counseling session were here because of me, because of someone I had been, their father or their sister or their friend. I was overwhelmed by a sense of loss so staggering that I knew I could never hope to overcome it or escape it. I tried to speak, but nothing came, and I shook my head helplessly. "What is there to say?"

"Whatever you want," said Rosie. She tilted her head to the side in a sympathetic gesture. "Who did you lose?"

"My wife," I said, repeating what I'd told her before.

"Would you like to tell us about her?"

There were so many, both young and old; sometimes I died first, and sometimes they died and left me alone. I stared at the floor, careful not to look at her, and tried to think of something to say.

I remembered another woman, barely more than a girl, a lifetime ago on the slopes of a great mountain. We lived in a hut of mud and thatch, watching a small flock of sheep on a field of short, stiff grass and twisted trees. She laughed freely, and she worked hard, and she died in childbirth, and I couldn't remember if I was her husband or if I was her. Maybe I was both, and her parents, and her child. I took so many back then.

Rosie and the others simply watched me, silent and supportive, giving me time to think before I spoke.

I opened my mouth, trying to think of a story they wouldn't recognize, a story Rosie wouldn't immediately see herself staring back from, but they were all the same: someone left, and someone else was left behind. The world was a broken puzzle, the pieces dumped out in a pile on the floor, close without ever being connected.

"Is it worth it?" I asked suddenly. I couldn't get that boy's words out of my mind. "We spend our whole lives making connections with people who are inevitably, every time and without fail, going to leave us. Unless we leave them first, which might actually be worse. We're building a foundation that cannot last, with materials that will never hold, and time goes on and mountains crumble and everybody dies, everyone and everything that ever was, and I...I am so old." I felt it then like I'd never felt it before, the sheer weight of my endless, ageless life, as deep and as black as a bottomless pit. It was age that ruined the Gifted—not time, for time was fleeting, but age itself. The relentless buildup of days and nights and days, of waking and doing and being and sleeping, over and over, forever. "Even my memories fade," I said softly, looking down at the keys on my lanyard, but Rosie stopped me with a single sentence.

"Do you feel that lasting—that staying, that remaining—are the only things that give something meaning?"

We'd thought that once, in the beginning. We wanted immortality, and we were willing to give up anything to get it. I don't remember what I'd given up, but I knew it was a part of me so deep, so central to myself, that I had never been the same person since. None of us had. We had reached for a gift, but we'd reached too far and we had withered instead, like dead vines shriveling in a glaring summer sun.

"Give meaning to what?" I asked, feeling bitter and empty. "If I give you meaning and you die, what good has it done?"

"You can't give me meaning," she said simply. "It's not yours to give; I have to do that on my own. Elijah, what has meaning for you?"

I looked at Rosie, remembering the day we were married, and the long nights we'd spent sick or worried or joyful in each other's arms. "People," I said.

"And what happened when those people were gone?"

I stared at her, so close I could almost touch her, and my voice came out in a strained whisper. "It is so much worse than simply being gone."

Rosie nodded, silent a moment, before speaking softly. "A life can be important because it affects other things, and it can have purpose because of what it accomplishes, or what it intends to accomplish, and those are active words. They have movement and life behind them, and when somebody dies, that life goes away, and it feels sometimes like the purpose and importance goes with them." Her eyes filled with tears. "Meaning is different. A life has meaning when it means something to someone else, and it can never do that on its own. It means something *to me*. To *you*. When that life is gone, it hurts us and it changes us and it feels sometimes like we're tearing apart, but no matter where that life goes, or if it even goes anywhere at all, the things that it meant are still there because it meant them to you. And as long as you hold that inside of you, it's not just *meant*, in the past tense, but *meaning*, in the present. Right now. You asked if making connections was worth it, and I promise you: it's the only worthwhile thing in the world."

*   *   *

I don't know what I was expecting from the meeting. A reunion, perhaps, though I knew it wouldn't happen. In years, maybe, when her loss had subsided.... But no. Even if she was ready, I wouldn't be the same anymore. I might even have forgotten her.

I forgot my way home and drove around in the middle of the night, thinking.

When I went to work again, the three Gifted were there, Gidri and Ihsan and the silent man. Ted was unconscious in the corner, his face bloody, and I ignored Gidri's cheerful greeting as I walked to Ted's body and leaned down to check his pulse and breathing. He was alive, but I couldn't imagine that the Gifted intended to leave him that way for long. I straightened and turned to face them.

"Is this your new plan?" I asked. "I won't join your army, so you kill my friend?"

"He's still alive," said the tall man.

"For now," said Gidri. "You know how the rest of this proposal goes, so I'll just sit and wait while you propose it to yourself." He sat on the edge of the desk, watching me with a dark, laughing gleam in his eye. Ihsan stood beside him, the scar on his face more prominent now than it was before, and in the corner the third man, sharp-faced and ominous, lurked like a shadow.

"Am I really that important to you?" I asked.

"You're our brother, Meshara."

"You've never cared about that before."

"How would you know?" asks Gidri, and the wicked grin that spread across his too-handsome face was all the more maddening, because I knew he was right: maybe they *did* care about me, and stood up for me, and I just couldn't remember it because I couldn't remember anything. I touched the keys on my lanyard and found myself reciting the litany of maintenance checks for the hearses. Did I still remember it all? Was I missing any steps? Ted would be able to help, but if I didn't tread carefully Ted would never do anything again.

"We want you on our side, because you're one of us," said Gidri. "You belong with us—with the whole Cursed family."

"Cursed?" I said, looking up in surprise. "I thought your side called us Gifted."

"I know a curse when I see one," said Gidri. "We wanted long life, assuming that it would be a good life by default, and we've had millennia to learn the truth of that mistake. But unless you're ready to roll over and die, what difference does it make? Even monsters can defend themselves."

I looked at Ted, unconscious and bloody. "From the big, scary humans."

"They're closer to winning than you think," said Gidri. "If we found you, they might have, too, and they could be watching us right now. Or someone else, maybe? Someone who's slowly inserted themselves into your life, gaining your trust, learning your secrets, waiting for the moment to strike."

I thought about Rosie, but there was no way she was hunting us. I knew her too well—better, literally, than I knew myself. She and Merrill and Jacob were the only people I knew. And Ted. Was that Ted?

I looked in the corner, and it was Jacob. Ted got a new job two years ago. Or was it longer?

I needed a new mind, and soon.

"You look confused," said Gidri.

"I'm fine."

"Your memory's failing," he continued. "You need a new one. As a token of good faith, allow us to provide one."

"Who?" I asked, but the tall man was already moving. I tried to step in front of Jacob, but he was too strong, and he pushed me out of the way like a doll and snapped Jacob's neck with his hands. "No!" I shouted, finding my voice at last, but it was too late.

"I'll need the skin when you're done," said the tall man, rubbing his scarred face, and his skin moved unnaturally across the bones beneath it, like a mask. I sank down at Jacob's side, feeling again for his pulse and breathing, but he was gone. I tried to remember how well I knew him, but I couldn't bring the thoughts to mind. Was he a stranger, or my best friend?

I felt the paranoia creeping in, triggered by the murder but rooted so much deeper. Every shadow was an enemy; every corner an ambush. When you can't remember what lurks beyond your peripheral vision, the world becomes a twisted, threatening madhouse.

I closed my eyes, rage fighting with despair. "You've lost now," I said, shaking my head at their callousness. "Jacob was my only friend, and you said if I joined you he could live. Now you have nothing to offer me."

"Don't be so sure," said Gidri, and the sharp-faced man slipped silently into the hall. Gidri smiled, showing his teeth, and my heart sagged, for there were only two other people they could hold me with. "You were gone an awfully long time," said Gidri.

"Please, no."

And then there she was.

The sharp-faced man dragged Rosie into the office, bound and gagged to keep her silent in whatever back room they'd hidden her. She was half awake and stumbling, her coat torn, her clothes disheveled, her scalp bleeding in ragged patches where someone had yanked or dragged her by the hair. I stepped toward her, but the tall man held me back, his hands strong as iron.

"Rosie," I said. She looked at me in foggy horror, still confused from being knocked unconscious.

"You see we still have plenty of leverage," said Gidri. He stood up and walked toward her. "Who is she, Meshara? Someone from a life you stole? Does she know what you are—or who you think you are?" He reached for her and she shied back, turning to run, but the sharp-faced man slammed his fist into the side of her face, knocking her to the floor. I surged forward, trying to protect her, screaming at Gidri to leave her alone, but Ihsan grabbed me from behind, wrapping me in a parody of a hug, restraining me with unholy strength. Rosie reached out her fingers, trying to crawl across the floor, and the sharp-faced man stomped on her fingers with a heavy black boot.

"Leave her alone," I said, as furious at myself as I was at him. It was my fault she was here, my contact with her, my stupid, selfish, reckless attempt to be close to her. They'd been watching me, and they knew I cared about something, and now they were using it against me. "I'll join your army," I said, "I'll do anything you ask, just let her go and don't ever touch her again."

"That started like begging," said Gidri, "but by the time you got to the end, it sounded suspiciously like threatening." He moved his finger, a tiny, almost imperceptible signal, and the sharp-faced man kicked Rosie in the ribs.

"Stop!" I cried, struggling like a madman. "What do you want me to say?"

Gidri put out his hand, and the sharp-faced man stopped, stepping back against the wall. Gidri crouched down and pulled the gag from Rosie's mouth, shushing her sobs and stroking her hair in small, soothing motions. "Shh. That's right. Just calm down. Tell us your name."

"Let me go," she said, curling up protectively.

"Just tell us your name," he said softly.

"Leave her alone," I said again, but he ignored me. She cringed back from the touch of his fingers on her face, but he touched her cheek again.

"Just your name," said Gidri.

"Rose," she said finally. Her voice was thick with fear.

"Have you lost someone close to you, Rose?"

"This is sick," I said. "Just let her go."

"You asked me what I wanted you to say," said Gidri, keeping his eyes on Rosie. "I want you to tell this Rose who you are." He looked up at me suddenly. "Who you are to her."

"I'm nothing." I tried to squirm out of Ihsan's grasp, but he held me too tightly.

"You are the opposite of nothing," said Gidri.

"I'm a god, then," I said desperately. "Is that what you want me to say? To take my place in your pantheon of monsters? I'm a god of death and fear," I said, each word splintering my heart into a thousand brittle shards, watching Rosie's face shift and wince in terror. "I am Meshara, the god of dreams and nightmares and memory."

"Who did you lose, Rose?" asked Gidri.

"Please, no," I said. I could never tell her that. Let her be scared of me and terrified of them and traumatized and damaged, but don't destroy her memory of Billy. Leave her that much at least.

"Tell her who you are," said Gidri.

I am the one who loves you more than anything in the world, I thought, *and I will protect you with my life*. I closed my eyes and leaned back against Ihsan, resting my head against his face. He shifted uncomfortably, not knowing how to react.

And then I began to drink.

I drew his memories through his skin like sweat, draining his mind in a rush that froze him in place, motionless and helpless. He forgot where he came from, what he was doing, and he let go of me. Thoughtless. He forgot where he was, and who. Selfless. He forgot how to stand, how to swallow, how to breathe, and collapsed on the floor in a heap.

"Holy Mother," said Gidri, and I leapt at him, grabbing him by the arm, and I wasn't just me but the tall man as well, an ancient warrior named Ihsan, a paragon of power too perfect for the world to endure, and I was great and I was glorious, and I was proud and scared and lost and tormented. Ihsan knew Gidri's plan, knew that he had a knife in his boot, and so when he reached for it I was ready, and I laid my hands upon his head and drained it like a bottle, and Gidri ceased to be anything but a twitching vegetable, and abruptly I remembered a hatred so powerful I dropped to my knees—hate for me, for himself, for the entire world. Gidri's memories squirmed through my mind like maggots, wriggling and biting and turning everything to filth, and then they sunk below the surface and were gone, lost in the fathomless depths of my mind.

The sharp-faced man rose up, erupting in a forest of angles and blades, slashing at me with a slick brown thorn that opened my chest like a razor. I fell back, reaching in vain to stop him, and I thought I heard voices in the hall. The sharp man turned, listening, and bounded suddenly through the door like a hound of hell. An abrupt thunder of gunfire stopped him in his tracks and shook him like a leaf, and as he fell, a man in black rushed into view to finish him off with a machete. Rosie was screaming, and I managed to pull myself to my feet, oozing ash and blood, and pull her into the corner behind me. Another figure in black, a woman with dark brown skin, rushed past the frenzied blade fight in the hallway and charged into the office, firing at me with a large caliber handgun. The bullets ripped past me, destroying the wall in a shower of wood and plaster. Rosie screamed again, and the woman with the gun stopped, holding the gun on us with unswerving aim, and spoke into the radio strapped to her shoulder.

"I have one still alive in here, but I can't hit him without hurting the woman."

"So try harder," said a voice on the radio, and I thought that I recognized it, but I couldn't tell from where.

"I need backup," the woman insisted. "He's healing."

I looked down at my chest, watching as the long, bloody gash slowly sealed itself closed. Thick black grime dripped from the wound and sizzled on the floor: soulstuff, withered and dark. I tried to speak, but my lungs were still reforming; I felt the bitter sear of ash in my throat.

"Please don't shoot us," said Rosie. She had no special reason to trust me, but she knew me better than these sudden invaders with guns and knives, so she stayed in the corner behind me.

The fight in the hall had drifted outside, but I could tell from shouts and roars and impacts that it was still raging. I wondered what kind of man could stand that long against a Withered. I looked back at the woman with the gun, knowing she could kill me if she tried, and praying that my lungs healed closed in time to defend myself.

And then the boy from the rest home appeared in the door, dressed in black like the others, and suddenly I knew why I had recognized the voice on the radio. Why was he here? What was going on? His eyes were alert and clever and dead all at once. He walked with a strange, almost trembling gait, as if restraining himself with every step, but I couldn't guess from what. His eyes roved over the bodies on the floor, the bloody mess of my chest, Rosie cowering in the corner, all with the same predatory detachment. He looked at me for a moment, silent, then slowly lowered himself to crouch over Gidri's body.

"You drained them?" he asked.

I frowned, confused. How could he possibly—

"He can only drain dead bodies," said the woman with the gun.

"Obviously not," said the boy, and touched Gidri's throat with a pale finger. "If they were dead, they'd turn to ash. That means he incapacitated them, and draining their minds is the only weapon he has."

The man with the machete reappeared in the hall, covered with greasy ash and bloody splinters. The fight was over, and he'd won. I felt a new wave of fear. These were the ones Gidri had talked about, the other side of our shadow war, and they were far more capable than I'd imagined.

"What are you talking about?" asked Rosie.

The woman with the gun ignored her, keeping the gun trained tightly on my chest. "Protocol says we kill him no matter what—"

"Protocol can wait," said the boy, and looked at me with renewed interest, the way one would look at an insect pinned to a board. "These aren't the first people you've drained without killing."

I felt a wave of shame, the deep, dark secret of a life I'd ruined, and I choked out an answer through my raw, ragged throat. "I never wanted to kill." My voice was scratched and painful, but I forced the words out. "I thought I could . . . sustain myself without hurting anyone, but it was all wrong. I never meant to hurt him."

"Who?" asked the woman.

"Merrill Evans," said the boy, and I felt again the horrible sadness of that night, desperate and barely sentient, when I'd searched for a mind and found only my friend, and I couldn't bear to kill him, so I'd tried what I'd thought was a mercy, and instead I'd damned him to a living hell. I sank to my knees, wishing I could forget, but this wrenching shame was the one thing I could never allow myself to lose. If I forgot what I'd done to Merrill, I might do it again to someone else.

"I have a shot," said the woman.

"Wait," said the boy, and turned to Rosie. "We're with a special branch of the FBI, and we're here to rescue you. We have an ambulance outside." He gestured at the woman with the gun. "Will you go with my friend, here?"

"Will you tell me what's going on?" asked Rosie.

"Outside," said the boy, and after a moment's hesitation Rosie stepped around me and took the woman's hand, moving toward the hall but then stopping in the doorway. The woman tugged on her arm, but Rosie paused to look at me one final time. She opened her mouth to speak, but then turned and left without a word. Another connection severed, another loved one gone forever.

The last little piece of my heart broke, and I looked back at the boy with the dead eyes.

"How did you know about us?" I asked.

"We have what you might call an informant."

"Another Withered?"

"Friend of a friend."

I nodded, watching the pieces slowly fit together, but there was still so much I didn't understand. "Who are you?"

"My name's John Cleaver," said the boy, and his dead eyes lit up with the hollow outlines of a smile. "Professional psychopath."

"Why didn't you kill me?"

"The war I assume Gidri warned you about is real," said John. He gestured at the carnage in the room. "I take it you didn't like his offer, so I'd like you to hear mine."

I remembered a starless night on an ancient mountain, and another offer that had doomed us all. Ten thousand years of loss and pain.

But I remembered Rosie, too. Our first kiss. A hundred thousand loves from a hundred thousand lives. I could hide, or I could give those lives meaning.

I closed my eyes, and dreamed of death.

When Dan was five years old he got autographs from both Darth Vader and Mr. Rogers. He owns more than 300 board games. He has visited fifteen different countries, and lived in three. He was diagnosed with hypochondria as a child, but it's mostly gone now. He memorizes poetry for fun. He will eat pretty much anything at least once. He collects ugly ties. He is terrified of needles, mediocrity, and senile dementia. When he dies, his wife has specific instructions to play Michael Jackson's "Don't Stop 'Til You Get Enough" at his funeral.

Visit Dan on the web at
www.TheDanWells.com

Printed in Great Britain
by Amazon